Once Upon a Safari

Story and
Illustrations
by
Pat Kim

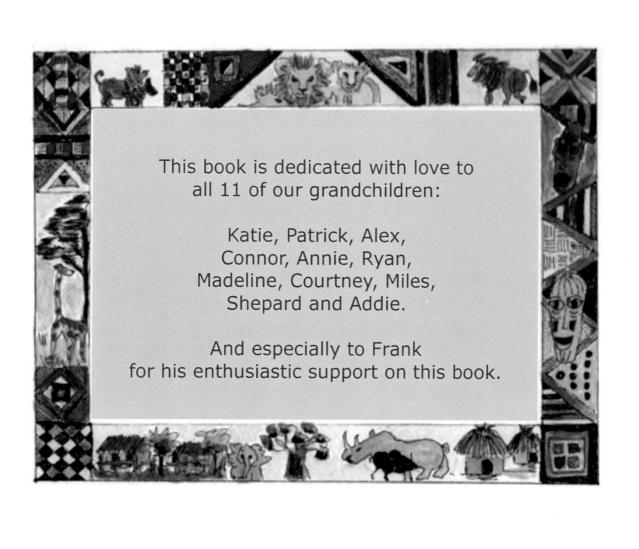

This book is dedicated with love to
all 11 of our grandchildren:

Katie, Patrick, Alex,
Connor, Annie, Ryan,
Madeline, Courtney, Miles,
Shepard and Addie.

And especially to Frank
for his enthusiastic support on this book.

"It's a home run!" Shep cried out.
"Wow! Look at it go!" Addie added.
"It's flying over the fence - all the way to Africa!" Po Po
exclaimed!

"Noooooo... It's my special Dodger's ball.
Andre Ethier signed it - my favorite Dodger,"
Shep said sadly.

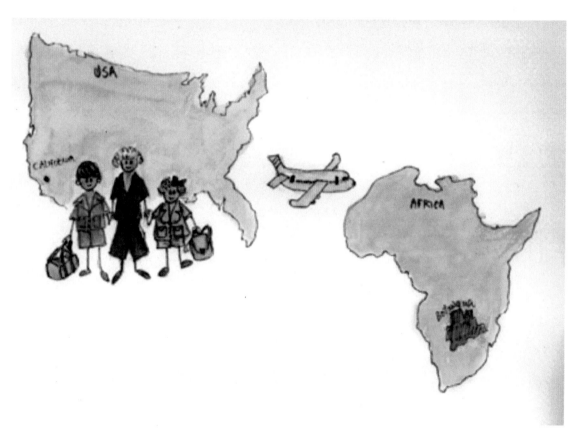

"We'll just have to go on a safari to find it,"
Po Po said.

We arrived at the Kalahari Desert in Botswana.
Our Bushmen guides met us in a Safari jeep
to take us to camp.

"Have you seen my baseball?" Shep asked after dinner.
"No," the porcupines said, busy eating table scraps

"Don't worry," the Bushmen said,
"We'll go to our village to see if other Bushmen
have seen your baseball."

"Look - a herd of kudus," the Bushmen stopped the jeep.

"Have you seen my baseball?" Shep asked.

"No," the kudus answered and continued on their way.

"No, we haven't seen your baseball," the onyx
answered. "What does it look like?"

The Bushmen found lion tracks... and led us to a
pride of lions.
"Have you seen a baseball here?" Shep asked.
"No," the papa lion answered with a loud roar.

"We didn't find the baseball at the Kalahari Desert," Po Po said to the Bushmen.
"We'll have to go to the Okavanga Delta to find it."
"Kalahari... Okavanga... in Botswana..." Addie said excitedly. "Oooh! I love saying those names."

"Hi, Elephants, have you seen my baseball?" Shep asked.
"No," the elephants replied.
"We are busy feeding on Mopani trees."

The Vervet monkeys said, "Nope! No baseball here.
But would you like to try a sausage from the
sausage tree?"

"Sorry! No baseball here!" said the giraffes.

"No, we haven't seen a baseball," the zebras replied.
"What is a baseball? Can we eat it?"

"No baseball here," the hippos said.

"Come into the river and swim with us."

"Watch out for the hippos," our guides warned us.

"Hippos kill more than any other animals in Africa."

"We haven't seen your baseball in the forest,"
chimed the warthogs.

"We've been in this waterhole all day. Didn't see any baseball," the wildebeests said.

"Haven't seen any ball here either on the savannah," the ostriches said.

"Haven't seen anything splash into the water.
Nothing but birds here by the river,"
the crocodile said.

"I'm the lilac-breasted roller - the prettiest and the national bird of Botswana. But I haven't seen your baseball from up this tree."

"It's getting so dark I can't see," Shep was getting
worried. "Is that a fire behind those trees?"
"That's only the fiery colors of an African
sunset," the Bushmen assured us.

"Be very quiet as we approach the cheetah," our guides said. "He has caught an impala for dinner."

"Turn off your headlights, " the cheetah growled. "Go away! Can't you see I'm having dinner? There's no baseball here!"

"No baseball flew over here," the wild dogs bared their fangs, "only the sparrow weavers building their nests across the river."

"Be careful of the wild dogs," the Bushmen warned. "They may be disappearing but they're ferocious."

"Didn't see anything! I just woke up." The African Cape Buffalo said, chomping on some grass.

"Nothing unusual here," the villagers said.
"Would you like to share our fish for lunch?"

"No baseball here!" said the white rhinos.
"But there's a lot of noise on the other side of the forest."

"Look! Shep!" Addie exclaimed.
"That baboon's got your baseball!"
"It seems the monkeys are having fun with your baseball," Po Po said.

"Hey! That's my baseball!" Shep pointed at the monkey. The monkey held onto the ball and just grinned. "But they're having so much fun! Why not just let them keep it?" Addie pleaded.

"Okay," Shep decided. "I will leave my baseball with the
monkeys in Africa. And maybe they will love baseball as
much as I do..."
"Well done, Children," Po Po smiled. "That's the spirit!
You can always get another baseball. And now, it's time to
go home."

THE END

Made in the USA
Las Vegas, NV
26 June 2022

50736491R00021